The Boy & His Balloon

By Eric Gates

ISBN: 9798496091442

Printed in the United States of America

First.

A baby is born.

He was a beautiful baby.

He grew and he played.

He became adventurous
and began to explore.

His favorite time were
walks to the park.

CENTRAL PARK

One day at the park he got a balloon and it made him happy.

He felt lifted.

He will always have a
balloon in his heart.

Time passed and he grew.

But one day...

He did bad,

and he felt bad.

He felt like he sank.

He will always have an anchor tied to his soul.

As the boy grew, the more good things he did...

the larger his balloon
grew,

and he floated higher.

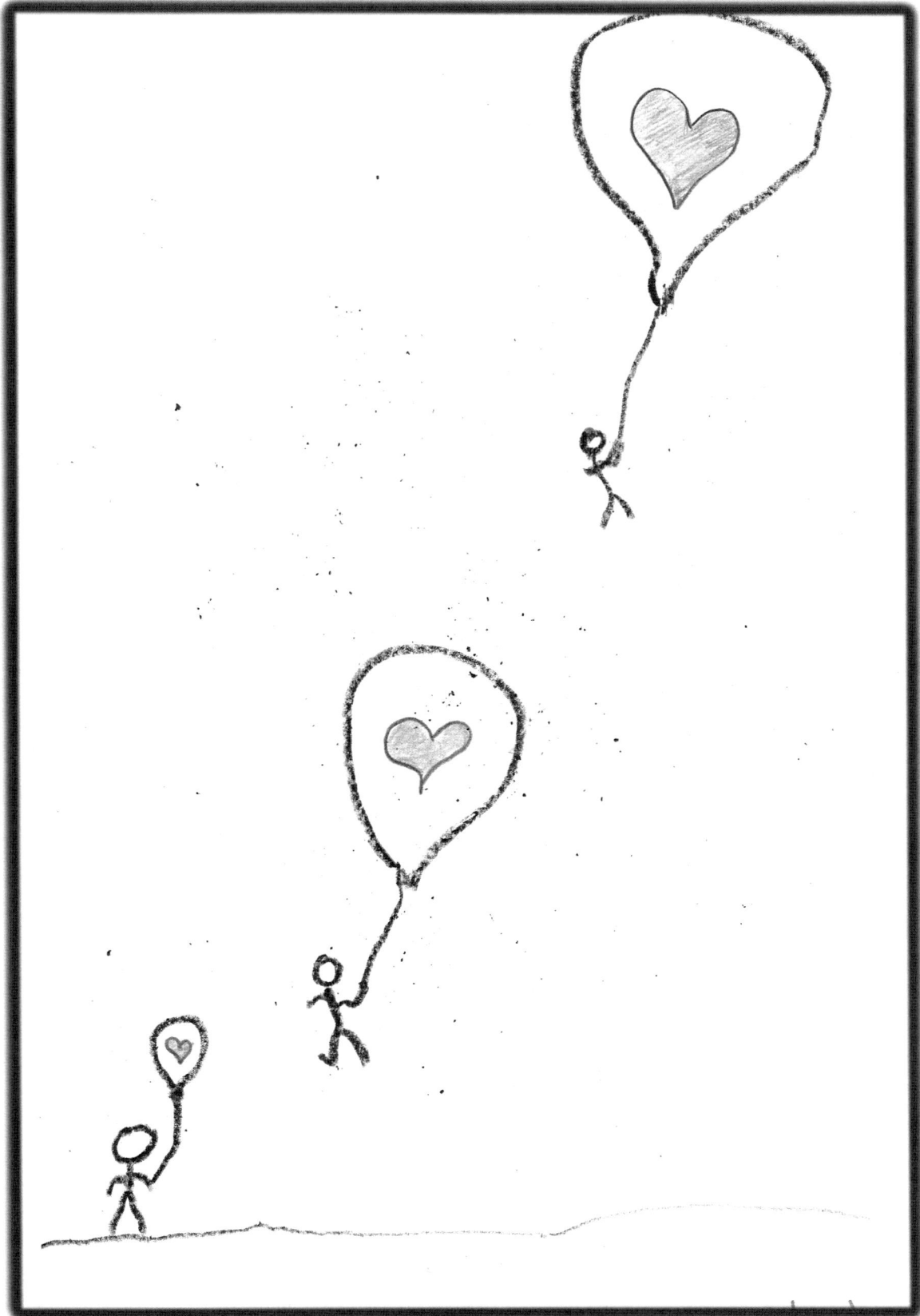

When he did wrong...

his anchor grew.

He carried them with him
wherever he went.

They were a part of him.

A balloon of happiness
tied to his heart
&
an anchor tied to his soul,
never to be put down
or ever let go.

Time passed,

and time passed,
and he grew.

He became a young man and needed a bigger balloon.

Up and away, he began his journey.

He floated along on his journey through life.

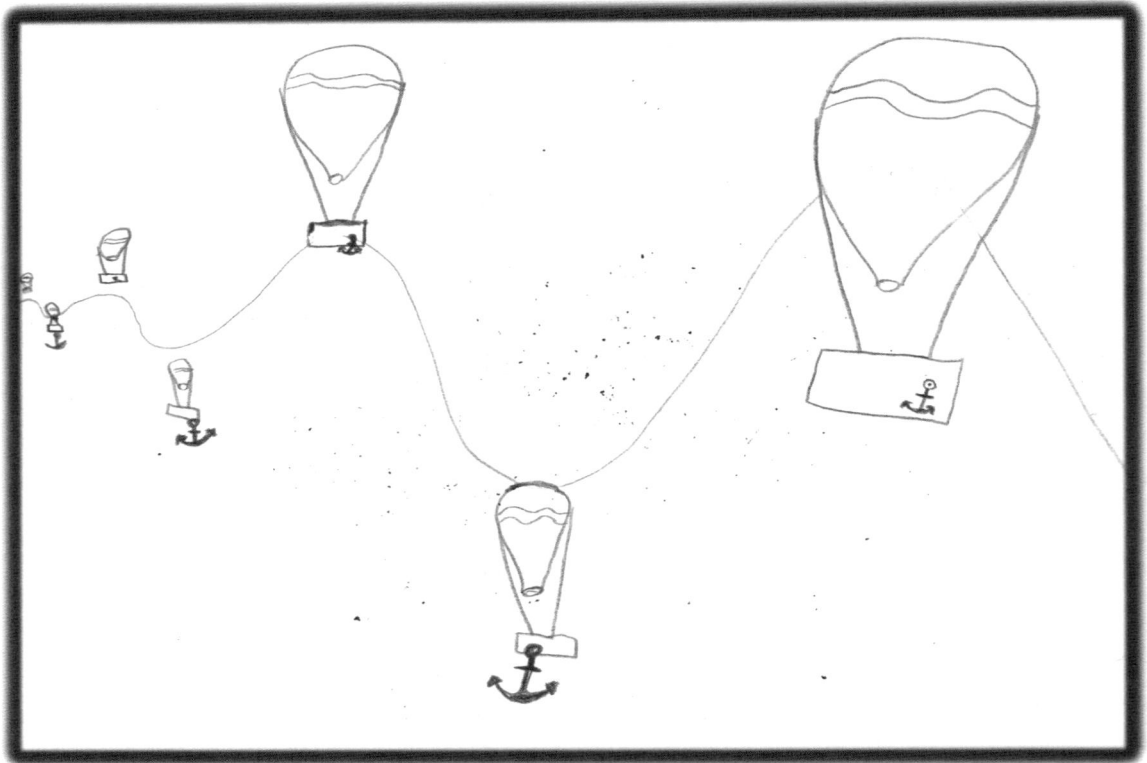

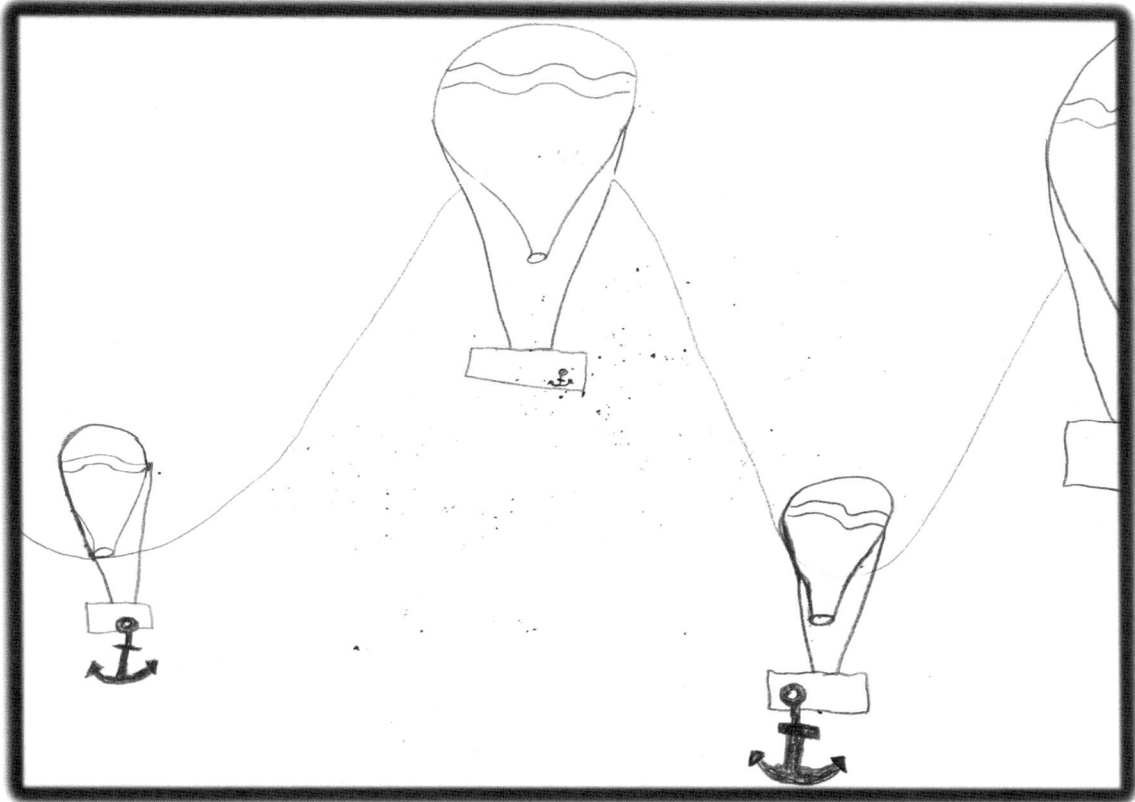

He added more to his basket...

and more...

and more...

He worked hard to lift the balloon.

He needed a bigger balloon.

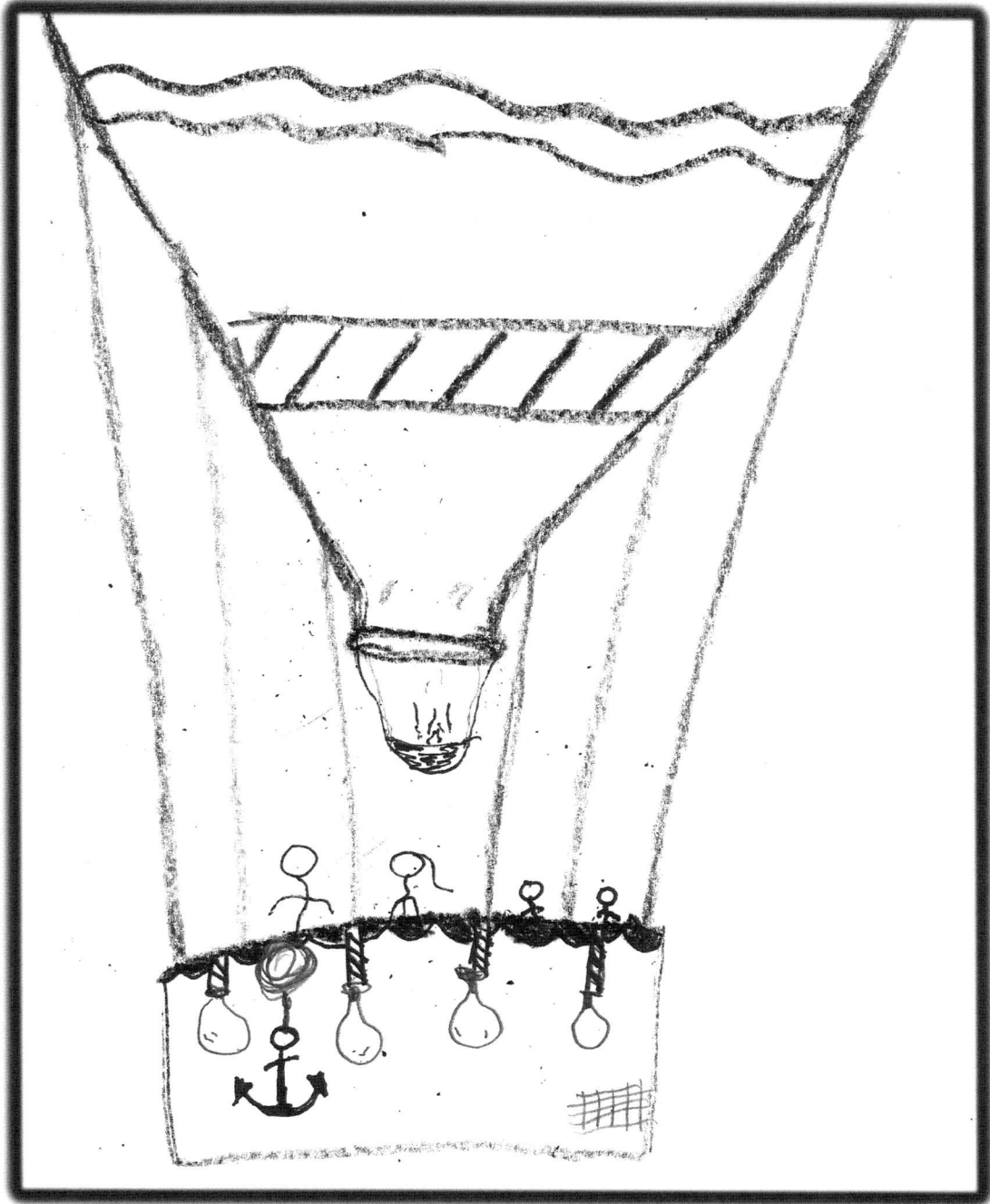

But he could never seem to rise any higher until he decided to drop a few sandbags.

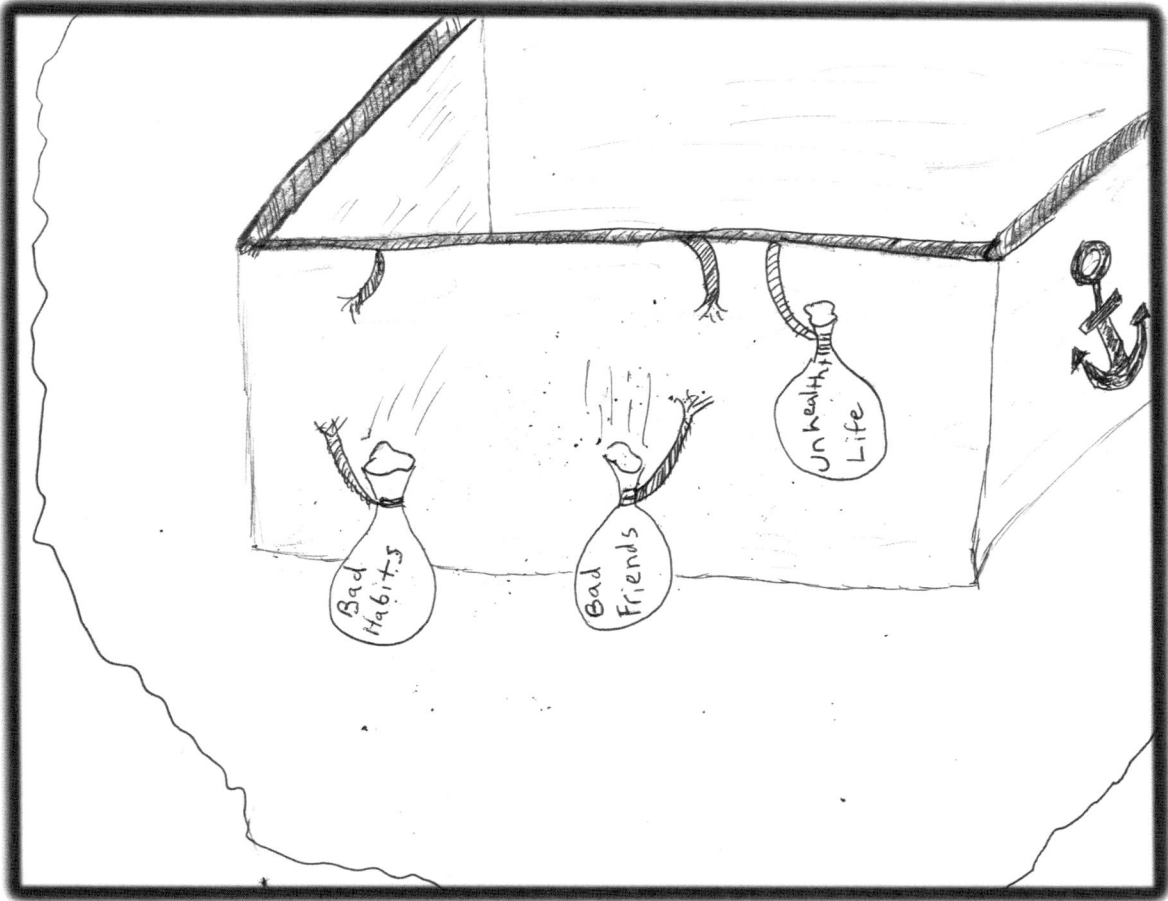

But still never lifting
very high.

Until one day he looked up,

and he realized it was
beautiful up there.

He was looking at the wrong thing.

He was focused on not letting his anchor hit the ground.

He realized he should have been looking up at his balloon.

So, he began to go to work.

And he lifted higher.

And found many more balloons.

There is a balloon of happiness tied to our hearts and an anchor attached to our soul.

As we do good our balloon grows. As we do bad, our anchor becomes heavier.

I can't tell you which one to focus on, but I have learned the happier I am the easier it is for me to lift and carry my depression.

Now I know that it is not always good,

and tragedies happen and it feels like your balloon is destroyed.

But if you survive the crash...

In time...

A new balloon will be born.

And if you work on it and nurture it...

it will someday be big
enough to lift the anchor
once again.

Made in the USA
Las Vegas, NV
24 November 2023